Please return/renew this item by the last
date shown. Books may also be renewed
by phone or internet.

🖥 www3.rbwm.gov.uk/libraries

☎ 01628 796969 (library hours)

☎ 0303 123 0035 (24 hours)

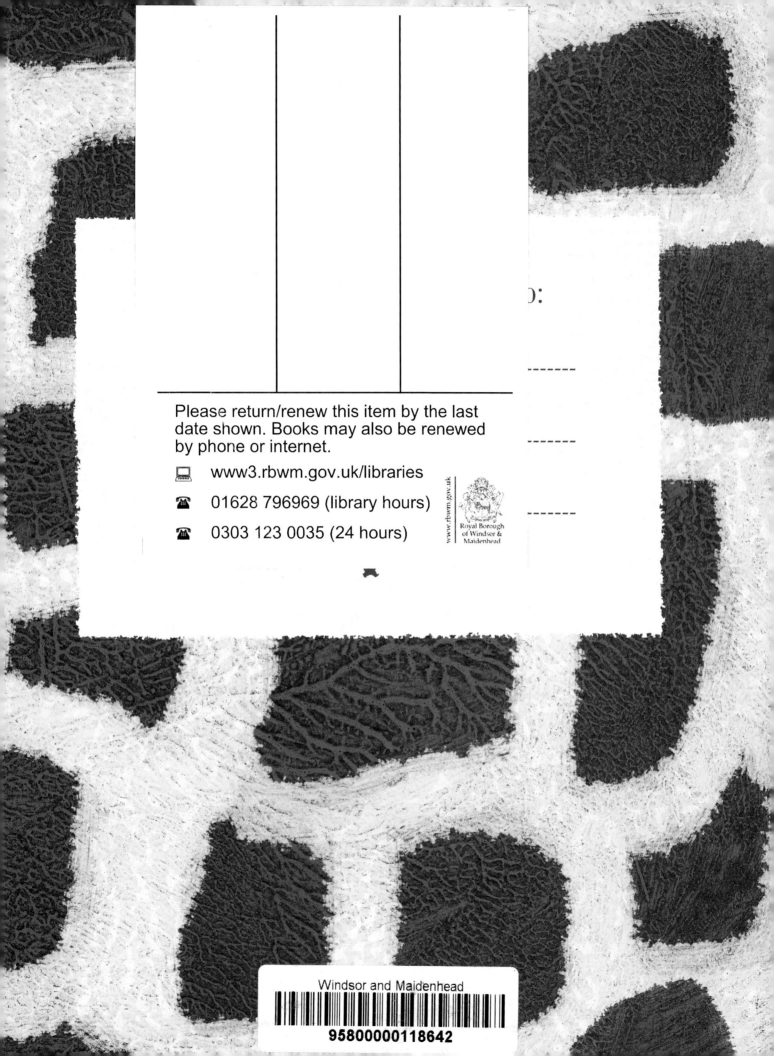

Royal Borough
of Windsor &
Maidenhead

www.rbwm.gov.uk

GIRAFFE PROBLEMS

BY **JORY JOHN** ILLUSTRATED BY **LANE SMITH**

WALKER BOOKS
AND SUBSIDIARIES
LONDON · BOSTON · SYDNEY · AUCKLAND

To Maria Modugno
~ J.J. & L.S.

First published in Great Britain 2018 by Walker Books Ltd
87 Vauxhall Walk, London SE11 5HJ

This edition published 2019

10 9 8 7 6 5 4 3 2 1

Text © 2018 Jory John   Illustrations © 2018 Lane Smith

The right of Jory John and Lane Smith to be identified as author and illustrator
respectively of this work has been asserted by them in accordance with the
Copyright, Designs and Patents Act 1988

Published by arrangement with Random House Children's Books,
a division of Penguin Random House LLC, New York, U.S.A.

This book has been typeset in Industrial736 BT and Lucida Grande

Printed in China

British Library Cataloguing in Publication Data:
a catalogue record for this book is available from the British Library

A tip of the hat to Nora Ephron

ISBN 978-1-4063-8563-2

www.walker.co.uk

Book design by Molly Leach

I feel bad about my neck.

I do.

I can't help it.

It's too long.

Too bendy.

Too narrow.

Too dopey.

Too patterned.

Too stretchy.

Too high.

Too lofty.

Too ... *necky*.

Yes, my neck is too necky.

Everybody stares at it.

This guy.

Him.

That guy.

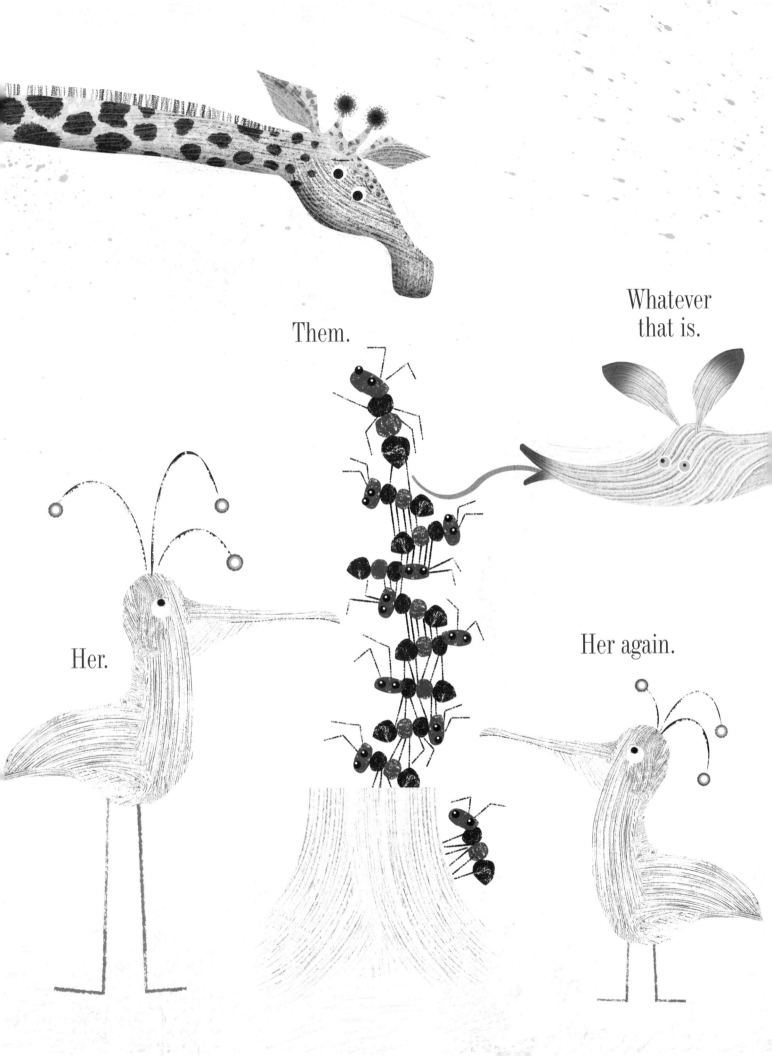

Them.

Whatever
that is.

Her.

Her again.

Yep, I feel bad about my neck.
I've tried dressing it up.

I've added a scarf.

Two scarves.

A bundle of scarves.

A *mountain* of scarves.

I've tried bow ties.

And regular ties.

And both.

I've tried hiding it away.
I've used shrubs.

I've hung out in ditches.

I've stood behind trees.

I've spent time in the river.

Other animals have necks that just ... *work*.
Take a gander at this zebra's neck.
Stripes *always* look good.
So classic.

Quit staring at me.

Or gaze upon this elephant's neck.
Strong and powerful, yet graceful.

Stop talking about me.

Or glimpse this lion, whose neck is adorned
with a glorious mane of flowing locks.

What a sight!

How inspiring!

Why can't I have a neck like THAT?

Are you *always* this loud?

My *mum* always said I should be *proud* of my neck.
She said other animals would *love* to have a neck like this.
Yeah, right.
No offence, Mum.
But *nobody* wants this neck.

It's a neck only a
mother could love.

It all makes me want to hide until the sun sets.

Sheesh.

Good evening…

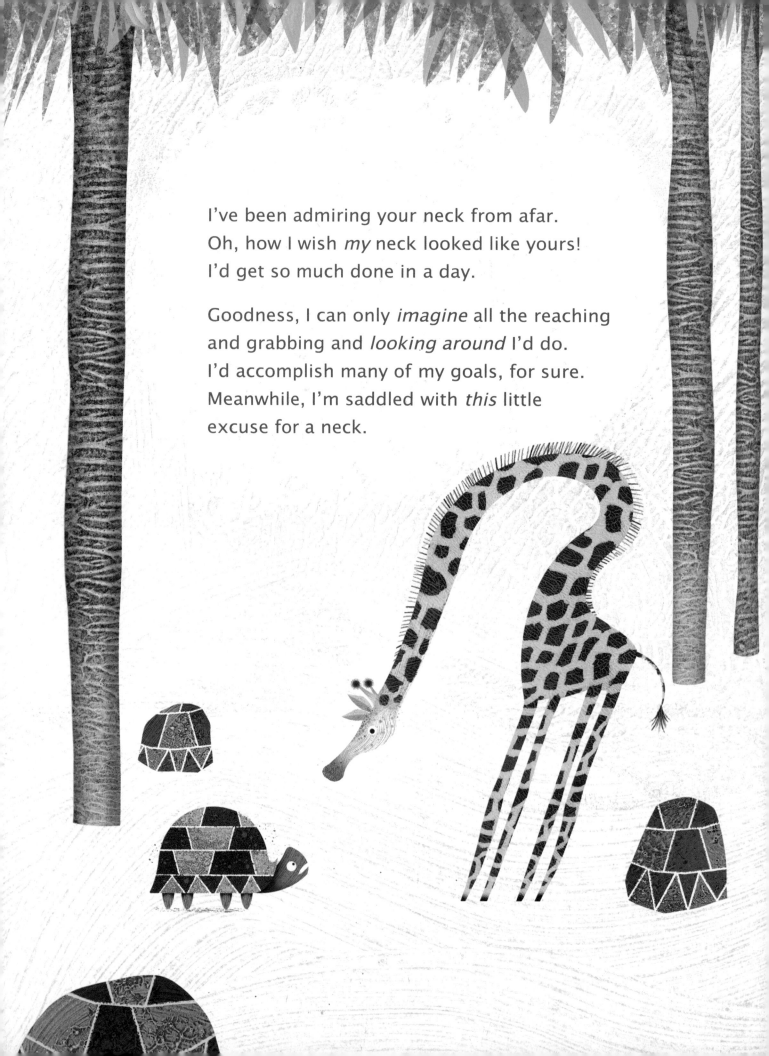

I've been admiring your neck from afar.
Oh, how I wish *my* neck looked like yours!
I'd get so much done in a day.

Goodness, I can only *imagine* all the reaching
and grabbing and *looking around* I'd do.
I'd accomplish many of my goals, for sure.
Meanwhile, I'm saddled with *this* little
excuse for a neck.

Here, watch me try to stretch it out.

Ugh.

See?
That's about as far as it goes.
Pathetic, right? I'm basically neckless.

Sigh.

Can I tell you something else, Edward?

Of course, Cyrus.

Ahem.

There is a hill in the distance, which you car

on that very hill for seven straight days now

fruit – a lone banana! – slowly changed from

nights and unseasonably brisk mornings, with

hoping against hope that the fruit would drop

nourish myself in the process. Yet, day after

neck towards those greedy branches, only to

surely see from your great vantage. I've stood

staring skyward, watching as a single piece of

green to yellow, ripening. I've endured windy

very little sleep, as I waited ... and *waited* ...

before me so I could sample its sweetness and

day, I've felt like such a fool as I stretched my

be limited by my own physical shortcomings.

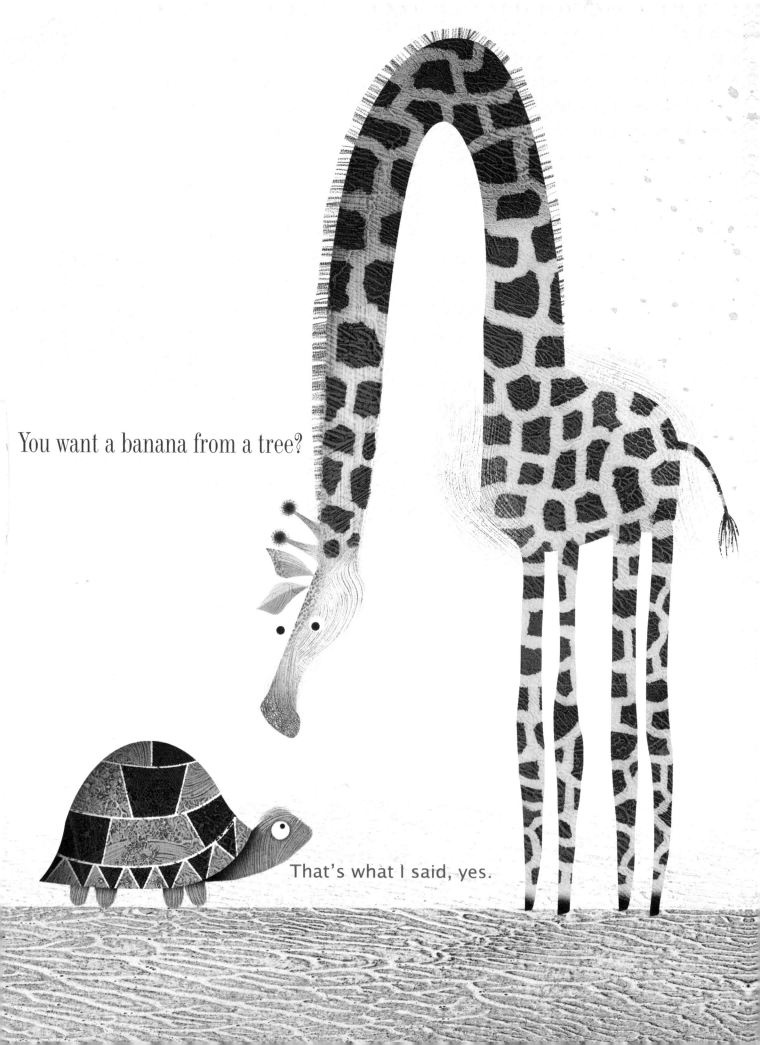

You want a banana from a tree?

That's what I said, yes.

PLUNK!

Here you go.

WHUMP!

Oh! You did it! You made it look so easy!

munch munch munch munch munch munch

Delectable!
So that's what a banana tastes like, huh?
It was worth the wait!

Edward, face it – your neck is impressive.
It allows you to do amazing things.
For instance, you just solved my weeklong
banana dilemma in ten seconds.

Well … thank you, Cyrus.
I think you have a swell neck, too.
It's elegant and dignified,
and it works well with your shell.

That means a great deal to me, Edward.

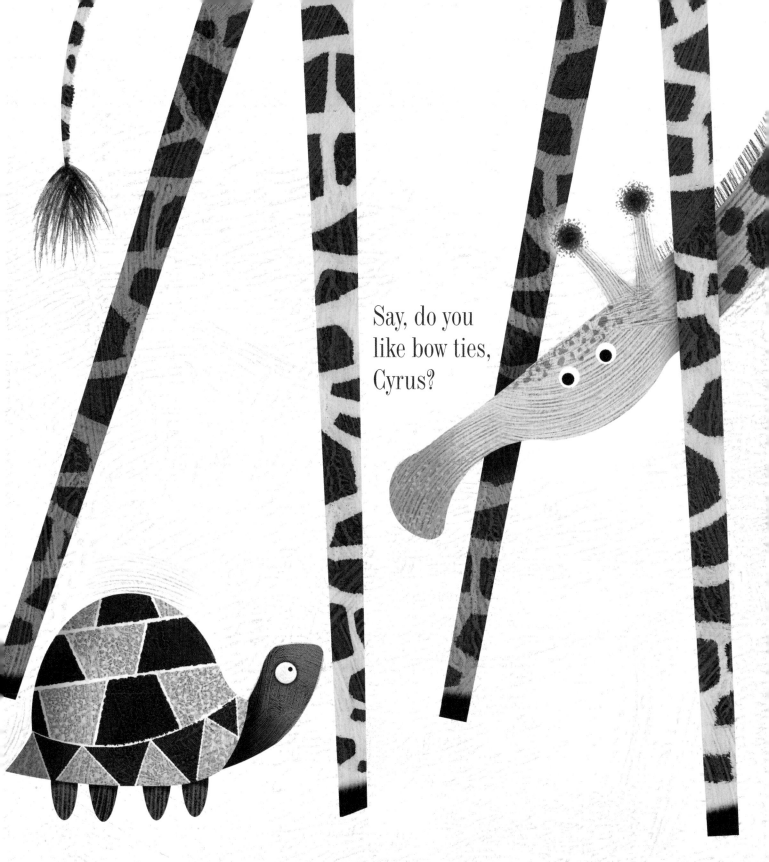

Say, do you like bow ties, Cyrus?

I'm ... I'm not *sure*, Edward.
I have very little experience with them.

You look wonderful, Cyrus!

As do you, Edward!

I feel good about our necks, Edward.

Thank you, Cyrus. For once, so do I. Yes, for once, so do I...